Two, Tree!

Anushka Ravishan— ao ❖ Durga Bai

TARA PUBLISHING

1

dizzy ant

One

dizzy ant totters up
the tree

2
dreamy lizards

Two

dreamy lizards
follow lazily

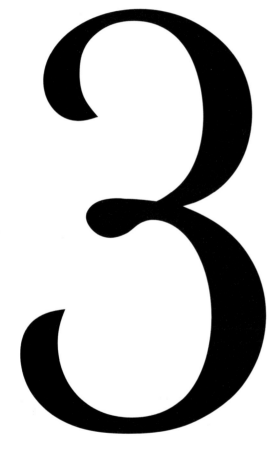

3
snoopy rats

Three
snoopy rats
run up to take a peek

4

goofy rabbits

Four

goofy rabbits
play hide and seek

5
grumpy dogs

Five
grumpy dogs climb
up and wonder why

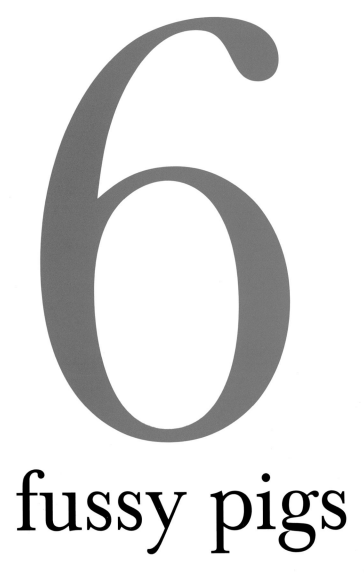

6
fussy pigs

Six

fussy pigs decide to
leave their sty

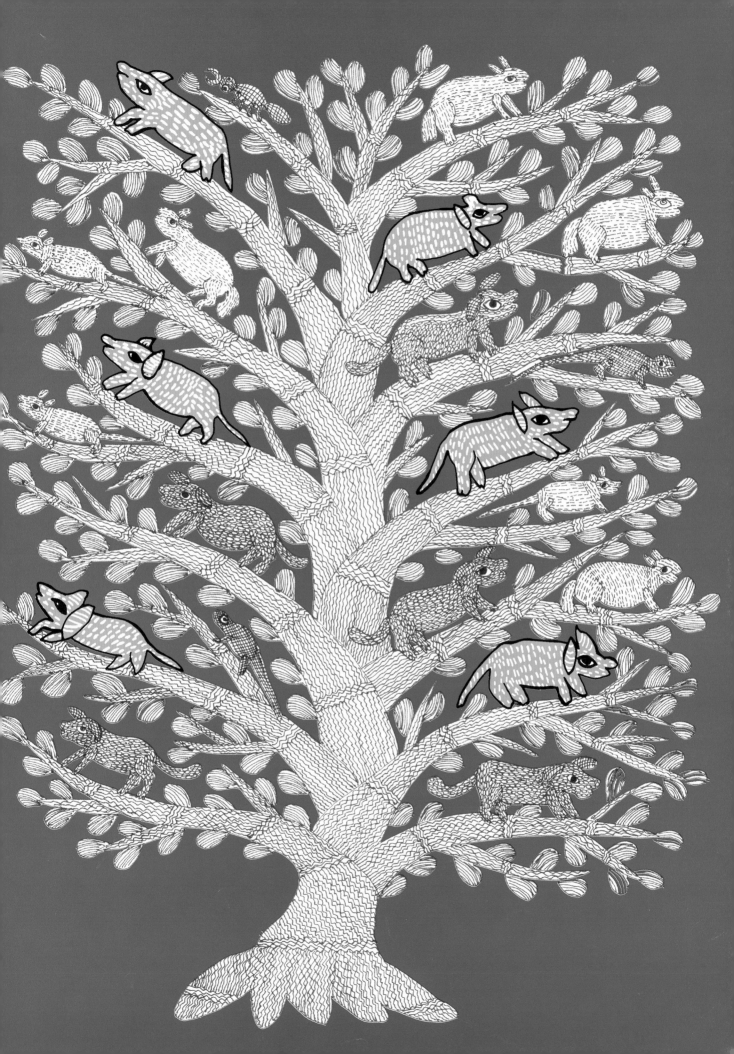

frisky deer

Seven

frisky deer butt in
without a word

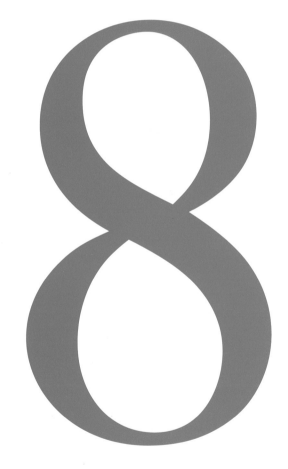

giggly hyenas

Eight

giggly hyenas find
the crowd absurd

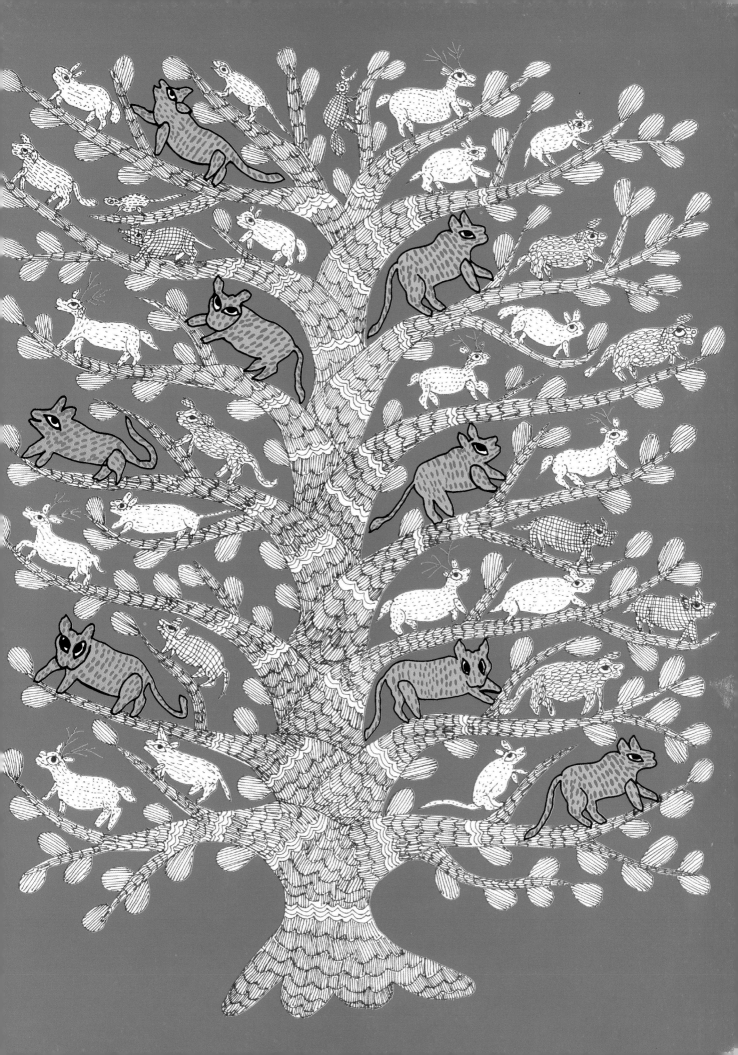

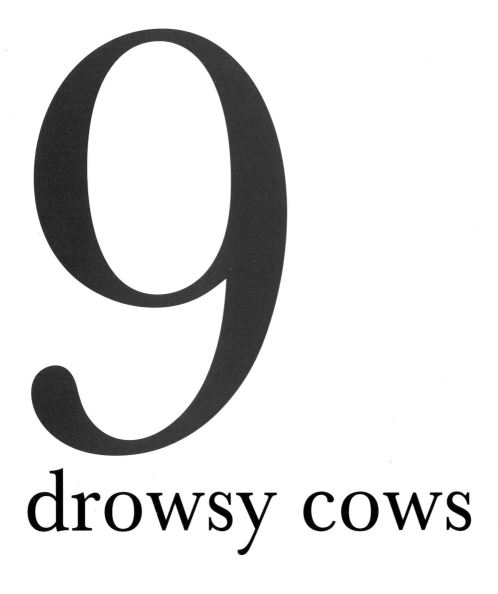

9
drowsy cows

Nine

drowsy cows
squeeze in and
start to snore

10
hefty elephants

Ten

hefty elephants...
Is there room for
more?

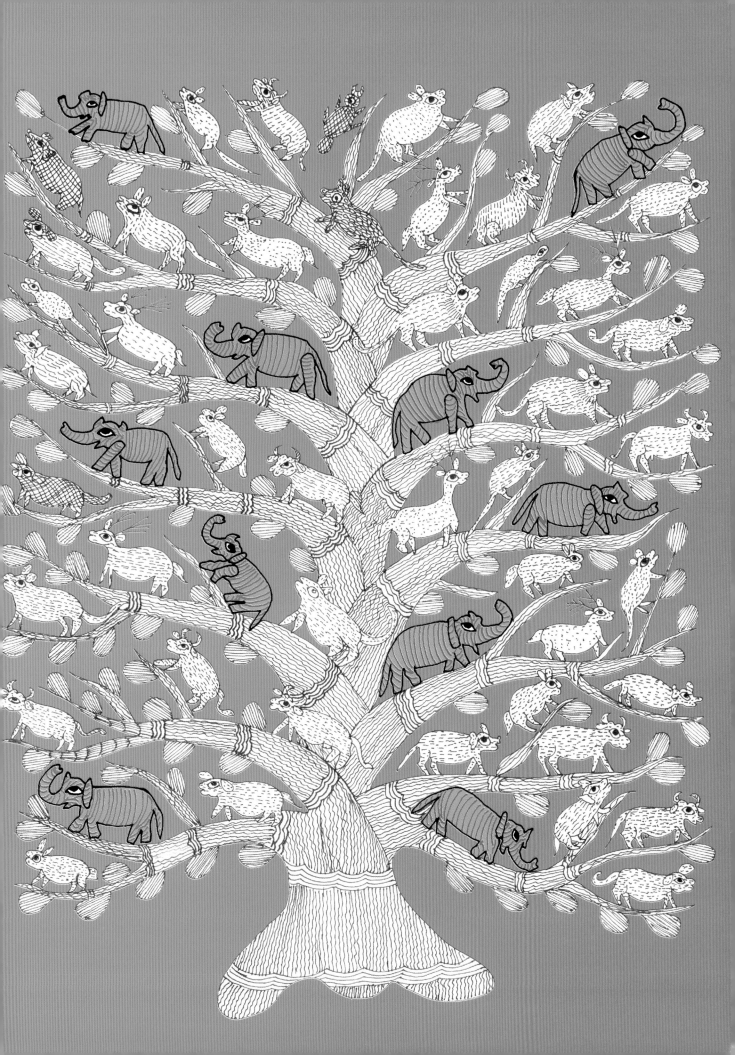

Let's hope so!

One, Two, Tree!
Copyright © 2003

For the text: Anushka Ravishankar, Sirish Rao
For the illustrations: Durga Bai

For this edition:
Tara Publishing Ltd., UK < www.tarabooks.com/uk >
and
Tara Publishing, India < www.tarabooks.com >

Design: Rathna Ramanathan, Minus 9 Design
Production: C. Arumugam
Printed in Thailand by Sirivatana Interprint PCL.

We would like to thank Kanchana Arni for her assistance with
this project.

ISBN: 81-86211-80-2

The Artist and Her Art

Durga Bai is a young artist from the Gond tribe in central India. Gond paintings are done on the walls of houses, showing scenes from everyday life and work, animals and birds, and the way human beings live in nature. Today, Gond art is also done on paper, and some artists have begun to paint scenes from modern life.

Durga's work is typical of the Gond tradition of painting, but at the same time, she enjoys experimenting and changing her style to suit her subject. Some of her best work has to do with the lives of women. She likes to show them in all kinds of familiar, yet unusual situations, from cutting grass and climbing trees, to playing football and swimming in waterfalls.

Durga is also very interested in understanding the larger social world around her. She has painted very moving scenes of suffering in the city of Bhopal - where she lives - when a gas plant leaked noxious fumes that killed and maimed thousands of people.

Eager to try something new with her traditional skills, she has now turned to book illustration. *One, Two, Tree!* is her first book, soon to be followed by others for Tara Publishing. She lives in Bhopal with her husband Subash Vyam.